Most Beloved Sister

Astrid Lindgren

Illustrations by Hans Arnold

Translated by
Elisabeth Kallick Dyssegaard

R&S
BOOKS

Stockholm   New York   London   Adelaide   Toronto

Now I'll tell you a secret that no one knows except me: *I have a twin sister.* Don't tell anyone! Not even Mama and Papa know. Because long ago when we were born, my sister and I—it was seven years ago—my sister jumped out right away and hid behind the large rosebush at the far end of the garden. Imagine—she could jump so far, even though she had just been born!

Do you want to know what my sister's name is? You may think that she's called Lena or Emma or some such girl's name. But she isn't. Her name is Lalla-Lee. Say it several times in a row, then you'll hear how pretty it sounds: Lalla-Lee, Lalla-Lee, Lalla-Lee.

My name is just plain Barbara. But
Lalla-Lee never says my name. She calls
me "Most Beloved Sister."
Lalla-Lee likes me so much. Papa likes
Mama best, and Mama likes my little
brother, who was born in the spring,
best. But Lalla-Lee just likes me.

Yesterday it was very hot. Early in the morning I went and sat behind the rosebush, as I usually do. It's in a corner of the garden where no one ever goes. Lalla-Lee and I have a special language, which only we understand. The rosebush has another name in our language. It's called Salikon. While I sat there next to Salikon, I heard Lalla-Lee call me: "Home cere!"

That's how you say "Come here" in our language. And I crawled into the hole. There is a hole in the ground right under Salikon. I crept in. Then I climbed down the long, long ladder and walked through the dark passage all the way to the door, which leads to the Golden Hall, where Lalla-Lee is queen.

I knocked on the door.
"Is that my Most Beloved Sister?" I heard
Lalla-Lee say inside.
"Yes," I said.
"Nicko, open the door for my Most
Beloved Sister," said Lalla-Lee.
And then the door opened, and Nicko,
the little dwarf who cooks for Lalla-Lee,
bowed and smiled just as he always does.

Lalla-Lee and I hugged each other for a long time. But then Ruff and Duff came running and began to bark and jump around us. Ruff and Duff are our small black poodles. Ruff is mine, and Duff is Lalla-Lee's. Ruff is always so happy when I come. He licks my hands and wags his tail and is so sweet. I used to beg Mama and Papa to get me a dog. But they said that dogs were expensive and troublesome and not good for my little brother either. That's why I was so happy to have Ruff. Lalla-Lee and I played with our dogs for a long time and had so much fun. Then we went to feed our rabbits. We have a lot of little white rabbits.

You'll never believe how beautiful
it is in the Golden Hall. The walls
shine with gold. In the middle of
the hall is a fountain with bright
green water. Lalla-Lee and I bathe
there.

When we had fed the rabbits, we
decided to go riding. Lalla-Lee's
horse is pale gold and its hooves
are gold, too. My horse is black.
Its mane and hooves are silver.
Our horses are called Goldfoot
and Silverfoot.

We rode through the Great Horrible Forest, where the Frights live. The Frights have green eyes and long arms. They rushed after us. They didn't say anything. They didn't scream. They just came up silently behind our horses and reached for us with their long arms. The Frights wanted to catch us and lock us up in the Great Horrible Cave. But Goldfoot and Silverfoot ran so fast that sparks shot up beneath their hooves—gold sparks and silver sparks. The Frights were left far behind. Later we came to the meadow, where the Kind Ones live. The Frights cannot go there. They must stay in the Great Horrible Forest. They stood at the edge of the forest and looked through the trees with their nasty

green eyes. We had such a good time with the Kind Ones. We jumped down from our horses and sat in the grass. Goldfoot and Silverfoot rolled in the grass and neighed. The Kind Ones, who have soft white clothes and red cheeks, came and gave us delicious cookies and caramels, which they carried on small green trays. No caramels are as good as the ones the Kind Ones make for us.

In the middle of the meadow the Kind
Ones have a large stove. That is where they
boil caramels and bake cookies.
Afterward we rode to the Most Beautiful
Valley in the World. No one may go there
except Lalla-Lee and me. The flowers sing
there, and the trees play music. A clear
brook runs through the valley. It can neither
sing nor play music. But it hums a melody.
I have never heard a prettier melody.

Lalla-Lee and I stood on the bridge that goes across the little brook, and heard the flowers sing and the trees play and the brook hum its melody. Then Lalla–Lee grabbed my arm very tightly and said, "Most Beloved Sister, there is something you must know!"

Right then, I felt a pain in my heart.

"No," I said. "I do not want to know."

"Yes, there's something you must know," Lalla-Lee went on. Then the flowers stopped singing and the trees stopped playing, and I could no longer hear the brook's melody.

"Most Beloved Sister," said Lalla-Lee, "when Salikon's roses wither, then I will be dead."

I threw myself up on my
horse and rode away from
there, and the tears ran down
my cheeks. I rode as fast as I
could. Lalla-Lee came racing
after me on her horse. We
rode so swiftly that Goldfoot
and Silverfoot were drenched
with sweat when we reached
the Golden Hall.

Nicko had prepared delicious pancakes for
us. We sat on the floor in front of the fire
and ate them. Ruff and Duff jumped
around us. Our rabbits also came hopping
up and wanted to be with us.
At last I had to go home. Lalla-Lee walked
me to the door. We gave each other such
a hard goodbye hug.

"Come again soon, Most Beloved Sister,"
said Lalla-Lee.
Then I went out the door and through
the passage and climbed up the ladder.
I heard Lalla-Lee call after me one
more time: "Come again soon, Most
Beloved Sister."
When I entered the nursery, Mama was

there putting my little brother to bed.
Her face was very pale, and when she
saw me, she left my little brother in the
crib and rushed over to me. She took me
in her arms and asked, "Dearest child,
where have you been? Where have you
been all day?"
"Behind the rosebush," I said.

"Oh, thank goodness, thank goodness you're here," said
Mama and kissed me. "We have been so worried."
And then she said, "Do you know what Papa has bought
for you today?"
"No, what is it?" I asked.
"Look in your room," said Mama.
As fast as I could, I rushed to look. And there, in a
corner beside my bed, lay a little black poodle puppy,
asleep. It awoke and jumped up and barked. It was the
sweetest dog I had seen in my life—yes, it was even

sweeter than Ruff down in the Golden Hall. It was as if it was more alive.

"It is yours alone," said Mama.

I picked it up in my arms, and it barked and tried to lick my face. Yes, it was the sweetest dog I'd ever seen.

"Its name is Ruff," said Mama.

Wasn't that strange?

I liked Ruff so much and I was so happy that I could barely sleep that night. Ruff lay in his basket beside my bed. Once in a while he whined a little in his sleep.

Ruff is mine alone.

This morning, when I went out into the garden, I saw that all of Salikon's roses had withered. And there was no longer a hole in the ground.